Calvin Can -
bE Happy

judy EdwaRd

Published by:

FriesenPress

Suite 300 – 852 Fort Street
Victoria, BC, Canada V8W 1H8

www.friesenpress.com

Distributed to the trade by The Ingram Book Company

ONCE UPON a tiME

iN a laNd faR, faR away

wHERE aNythiNG was possiblE...

tHERE livEd a boy NaMEd calviN.

Calvin was happy.

He was playing with his building blocks.

"look what i made mama!

a house

and a truck

and a car."

"you are a very good builder" said mama.

"i REally liKE tHE tHiNGS you MaKE."

"but now it's time to put the building blocks away.

it's time to get ready for school."

"oh my" said mama. "i thought you liKEd school."

"i do liKE school" said calviN.

"but RiGHt Now i waNt to play
with my building blocks."

"i uNdERstaNd" said MaMa.

"but SoMEtiMES WE haVE to CHaNGE what WE aRE doiNG.

SoMEtiMES WE haVE to Stop playiNG So WE caN GEt REady to do SoMEthiNG ElSE."

"No!" yelled calvin.

"i don't want to!"

and he stamped his foot and made a big frowning face.

"dEaR ME" Said MaMa.

"wE HavE to GEt REady foR School,
aNd you looK vERy uNHappy.

what will wE do?"

"i doN't KNow" said calviN.

"i havE aN idEa" Said MaMa

"WHy doN't you JuSt dEcidE to bE HaPPy?"

"you can't just decide to be happy" said calvin.

"WEll i thiNK WE ShoUld GiVE it a tRy" Said maMa.

"HoW?" aSKEd CalviN.

"HMM – lET'S StaRt by MaKiNG a biG SMilEy FacE" Said MaMa.

calvin tRiEd to SMilE.

at fiRSt HiS FacE didN't waNt to SMilE.

So maMa smilEd fiRst.

Calvin looked at mama. then
He tried again...

at first His smile was very small.

tHEN it Got a littlE biGGER.

MaMa SMilEd back at HiM.

THEN HiS SMilE Got EvEN biGGER

aNd biGGER

aNd biGGER.

Then calvin and mama laughed
out loud together.

"you SEE!" said MaMa.

"SOMEtiMES if WE just dECidE to bE HaPPY, it CHaNGES EVERYtHiNG."

"i SEE" said calviN. "i thiNK that just
FoR today i will dECidE to bE happy."

MaMa SMilEd aGaiN.

"wHo caN dEcidE to bE Happy?" SHE asKEd.

"calviN caN!" SHoutEd calviN.

"EvERyonE caN" SMilEd mama.

CPSIA information can be obtained
at www.ICGtesting.com
Printed in the USA
LVIC091034300912
300875LV00004B

9 781460 200971